What Makes Me SPECIAL

A Neurodiverse Child's Journey

Written by **Claudia Rose Addeo**

Illustrated by **Adam Gordon**

Scan the QR code with your phone camera to find more titles like this from
Imagine and Wonder

Your guarantee of quality

As publishers, we strive to produce every book to the highest commercial
standards. The printing and binding have been planned to ensure a sturdy,
attractive publication which should give years of enjoyment. If your copy
fails to meet our high standards, please inform us and we will gladly replace
it. admin@imagineandwonder.com

Printed in the USA

Dedications

To the strongest woman I know…my mother.

Mom,
Thank you for teaching me how to use my voice.
You always told me I could be anything or anyone I wanted to be when I got older…
but the only person I wanted to grow up to be was you.

Dad,
My knight in shining armor since day one…
Thank you for always being the best father and my hero.

Carrie,
Thank you for being on this journey with me…
I wouldn't be here without you.
You truly are the best of the best.

Everyone always tells you how special you are when you're little.
I mean I know I'm special, but the thing is, what makes me special?

I know I'm special. I know I am, because even Mommy and Daddy say so. I'm special because I don't like the way my birthday hat feels on my head, so Mommy and Daddy each wear one for me on my birthday!

I'm special because there is no other me out there.

I'm special because I have curly, light brown hair and big, round brown eyes. I used to feel insecure about this, because the kids in school would say my hair reminded them of a poodle, and my eyes were big and round, like a fish.

I always wanted to fit in with the other kids, and I always had friends...but I also knew these were just some things that made me special, just like Mommy and Daddy said.

I'm special because I didn't start speaking until I was four years old. Mommy and Daddy were so happy the first time I spoke.

I saw a flag while Mommy, Daddy and I were driving in the car, so I pointed to it and said, "flag." I said it again and Mommy started to cry, but she told me she had happy tears in her eyes. This is just another thing that makes me special.

I'm special, because I get pulled out of my classroom during the school day to go to special classes. Some of these special classes are resource room, speech class, occupational therapy, and I even get extra time one-on-one with the gym teacher too!

This is how I know I'm very special. If only the other kids were able to do all the fun things, I get to do...then they could be special too!

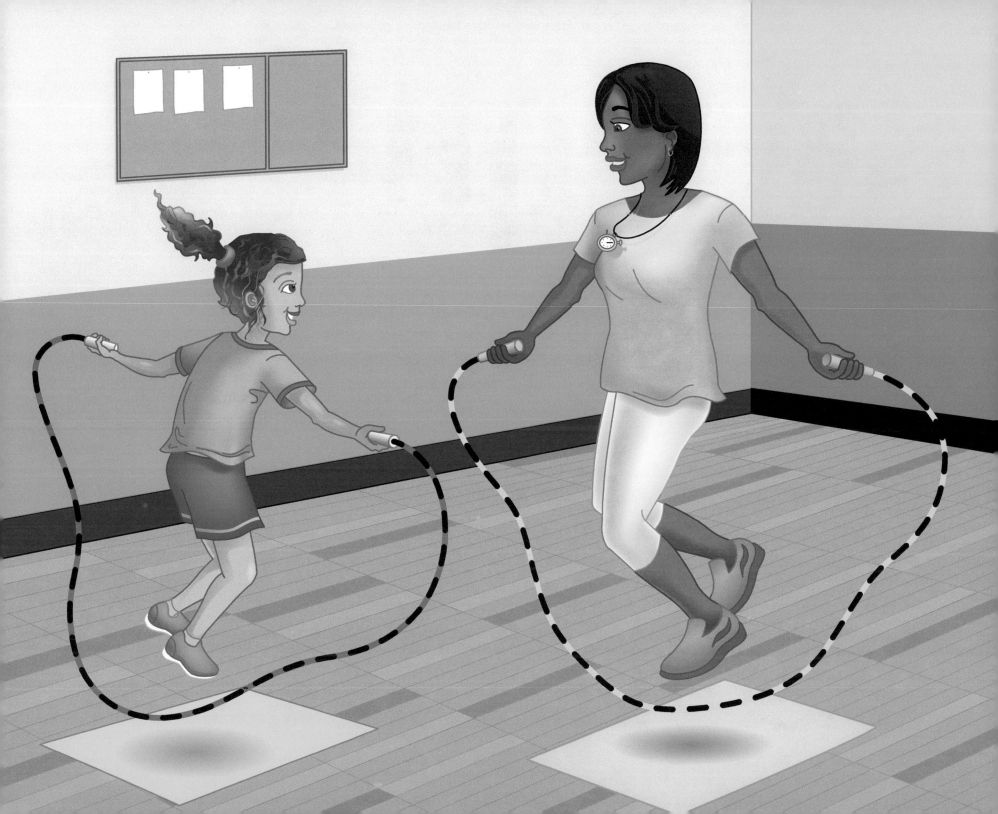

I'm special because I get to see my favorite tutor, Carrie! I see Carrie every day after school, and even on Saturdays. We always do schoolwork, but I also get a reward or get to pick out a game to play every time we finish doing schoolwork together.

I like when Carrie comes over. Carrie always gives me compliments which makes me feel so good!!! After I hear these nice things, it makes me want to work even harder. I really like Carrie because she understands just how special I am.

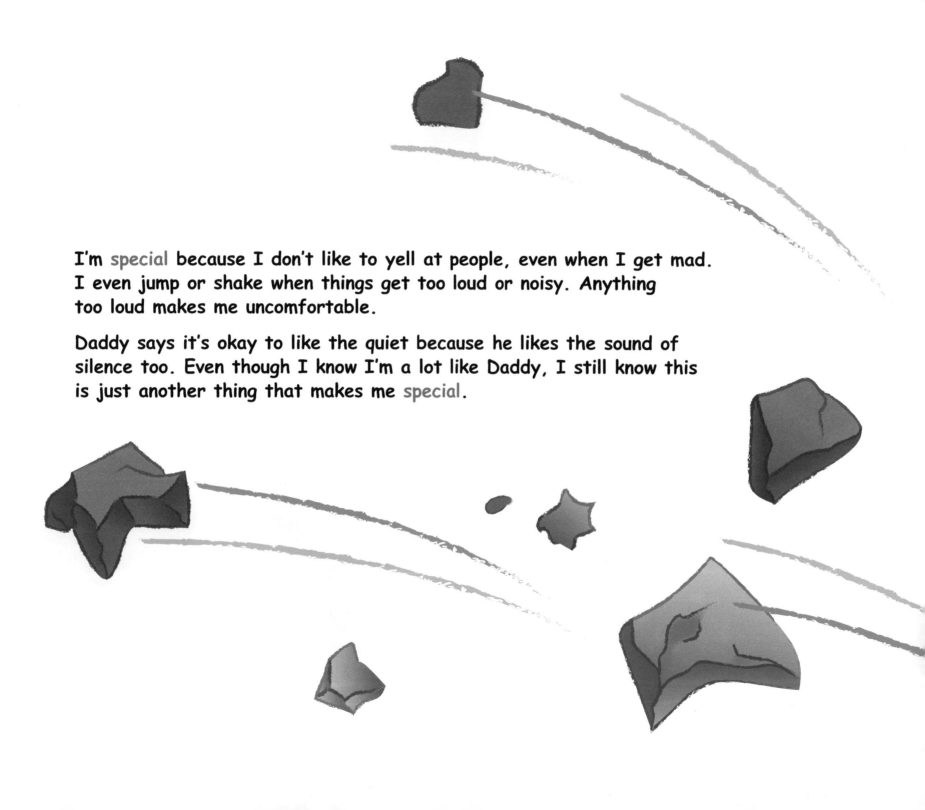

I'm special because I don't like to yell at people, even when I get mad. I even jump or shake when things get too loud or noisy. Anything too loud makes me uncomfortable.

Daddy says it's okay to like the quiet because he likes the sound of silence too. Even though I know I'm a lot like Daddy, I still know this is just another thing that makes me special.

I'm special because I have a hard time focusing. Mommy says it's my job as a hard worker to bring myself back on task whenever I zone out during class. Sometimes, it's extra hard for me to bring myself back on task.

When teachers only talk to me, I tend to zone out. Mommy says I'm daydreaming. I like when teachers use pictures to teach me or explain something to me, because it's a lot easier for me to pay attention. This is just another thing that makes me special.

I'm special because I don't see any differences between me and the other kids in school. I just see them as children just like me because...aren't we all the same on the inside? At least that is what I have always believed.

Mommy says this is one of the things that makes me her very special gift. Mommy always knows how to make me feel extra special in the best way possible.

I'm special because I always say please and thank you and try to be kind to others. I even try to be kind to strangers. When I go to school, the teachers are always saying, "treat others the way you want to be treated."

I feel uncomfortable being mean or unfriendly to other people. I always feel really good inside when I help others even when I don't know them, because it is the right thing to do. Grandma says this is what makes me very special.

I'm special because I always get extra time on tests. I have to study extra hard just to keep up with the other kids, but I always feel proud of myself when I get a good grade. Sometimes, I struggle and get angry. Sometimes, I even cry because I have such a hard time with school.

Mommy and Daddy say that's okay because I'm the hardest worker they know, and they'll always be proud of me as long as I try my best. Mommy and Daddy say that is just another thing that makes me special.

I'm special because even though I have a really hard time in school, I'm good in art class. My grandma says I could be an artist, that's how good I am in art class. Mommy says this is one of the many things that makes me her special gift.

I like that I don't have to try so hard or struggle when I'm in art class. Art comes a lot easier to me, and I know that is just another thing that makes me special.

I'm special because I get to go to the annual picnic my elementary school hosts at the end of each school year. The picnic is only for the kids who get pulled out of class for Resource Room, like me! I like that because a lot of the kids there are special, just like me.

I feel so lucky that I get invited to this picnic every year because all my favorite teachers go to the picnic! I know this is just another thing that makes me special, but I'm thinking my teachers might be special too.

I'm special because I have a big family. I have almost twenty first cousins and a lot of aunts and uncles. Some of my aunts and uncles are Mommy and Daddy's friends, but I still call them aunt and uncle. I learned that family does not always have to be related to you.

Sometimes, the best family members are the ones you are not related to, but they are still part of your family.

All my family members know how special I am, and they are always there for me. My big family always makes me feel good about being special.

My grandma says everyone always wants what they can't have, so I should feel very lucky for what I have. My grandma always reminds me of how lucky I am to be special.

There are a lot of things that make me special. I am special because of the way I walk. I am special because of the way I talk. I am special because of the way I work in school. These are just a few of the many things that makes me special.

Enough about me, what's special about YOU?